Dear Parents:

Congratulations! Your child is taking the first steps on an exciting journey. The destination? Independent reading!

STEP INTO READING® will help your child get there. The program offers five steps to reading success. Each step includes fun stories and colorful art or photographs. In addition to original fiction and books with favorite characters, there are Step into Reading Non-Fiction Readers, Phonics Readers and Boxed Sets, Sticker Readers, and Comic Readers—a complete literacy program with something to interest every child.

Learning to Read, Step by Step!

Ready to Read Preschool–Kindergarten
• big type and easy words • rhyme and rhythm • picture clues
For children who know the alphabet and are eager to begin reading.

Reading with Help Preschool–Grade 1
• basic vocabulary • short sentences • simple stories
For children who recognize familiar words and sound out new words with help.

Reading on Your Own Grades 1–3
• engaging characters • easy-to-follow plots • popular topics
For children who are ready to read on their own.

Reading Paragraphs Grades 2–3
• challenging vocabulary • short paragraphs • exciting stories
For newly independent readers who read simple sentences with confidence.

Ready for Chapters Grades 2–4
• chapters • longer paragraphs • full-color art
For children who want to take the plunge into chapter books but still like colorful pictures.

STEP INTO READING® is designed to give every child a successful reading experience. The grade levels are only guides; children will progress through the steps at their own speed, developing confidence in their reading.

Remember, a lifetime love of reading starts with a single step!

Disney Princess

Five Enchanting Tales

Step into Reading, Random House, and the Random House colophon are registered trademarks
of Penguin Random House LLC.

Visit us on the Web!
StepIntoReading.com
randomhousekids.com

Educators and librarians, for a variety of teaching tools, visit us at
RHTeachersLibrarians.com

ISBN 978-0-7364-3518-5

MANUFACTURED IN CHINA   10 9 8 7 6 5 4

Random House Children's Books supports the First Amendment and celebrates the right to read.

STEP INTO READING®

STEP 2
READING WITH HELP

DISNEP
PRINCESS
Five Enchanting Tales

Step 2 Books

A Collection of Five Early Readers

Random House 🏠 New York

Contents

Kiss the Frog

by Melissa Lagonegro

illustrated by Elizabeth Tate, Caroline LaVelle Egan,
Studio IBOIX, Michael Inman, and the Disney Storybook Artists

Random House 🏠 New York

Tiana works hard.

She has no time

for fun.

She has a dream.

She wants to own

a restaurant.

Prince Naveen
likes to have fun.

He loves music.

He visits New Orleans.

Facilier is a bad man.

He plans to trick

Naveen.

Facilier uses bad magic.

He turns Prince Naveen

into a frog!

Tiana goes
to a costume party.
She wishes on a star.
She wishes
for her restaurant.
Naveen sees her.

Tiana meets Naveen.
She looks like a princess.
Naveen thinks her kiss
will make him human.
He wants to kiss Tiana.

Tiana kisses Naveen.

But she is not

a real princess.

The kiss does not work!

Naveen is still a frog.

Tiana turns

into a frog,

too!

Tiana and Naveen
get lost.
They do not like
being frogs.
They do not like
each other.

They meet
Louis the alligator.
Naveen has fun!
Tiana does not.

The frogs try
to catch a bug.
They get stuck together.

Ray is a firefly.

He helps the frogs.

They all become friends.

Tiana shows Naveen

how to cook.

They like
each other now.

Tiana and Naveen
find Mama Odie.

She makes good magic.

She can help them.

Mama Odie

shows Naveen

a princess.

He must kiss her.
Then he and Tiana will
become human again!

Tiana and Naveen
are happy!
They are in love.

Naveen kisses a princess.

But it is too late.

The spell does not break!

Naveen is still a frog.

Tiana is still a frog.

Tiana and Prince Naveen
go back to Mama Odie.
They get married.

Now Tiana is

a <u>real</u> princess.

They kiss. <u>POOF!</u>

They become human again!

Tiana's dream comes true.

She gets her restaurant.

She has love.

She has everything she needs!

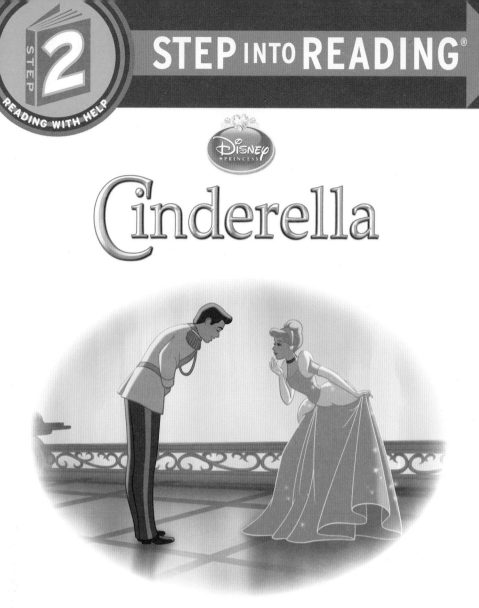
Cinderella

by Melissa Lagonegro

illustrated by the Disney Storybook Artists

Random House 🏠 New York

Cinderella is a kind
and pretty girl.
She has many
animal friends.

Cinderella lives
with her mean
stepfamily
and their nasty cat.
She does all the chores.
The stepsisters yell
at Cinderella.

Cinderella's stepmother
is Lady Tremaine.
She does not like
Cinderella.

She gives Cinderella
more chores to do.

The family gets a letter.
The Prince is having
a royal ball!

Everyone in the kingdom
is invited.
Cinderella must finish
her chores
before she can go.

Cinderella finds
an old dress
in the attic.
She can fix it.

She can make it pretty!
Cinderella
and her friends
are excited.

Lady Tremaine gives
Cinderella a pile
of clothes to sew.

Cinderella's friends
fix her dress for her.
The birds add bows.
The mice add ribbons
and beads.

Surprise!
Cinderella loves
her new dress.
Her chores are done.
She can go
to the ball!

53

Cinderella looks pretty.
Her stepsisters are mad.

They do not want
Cinderella to go
to the ball.
They tear her dress
and pull her beads.

Cinderella is sad.
The Fairy Godmother
appears.

She turns a pumpkin
into a coach.
It will take Cinderella
to the ball!

The Fairy Godmother
gives Cinderella
a sparkling dress
and glass slippers.

Cinderella is ready
for the ball!
She must be home
before the magic stops.

Cinderella arrives
at the palace.

She meets the Prince.

He asks her to dance.

They take a walk.

They fall in love.

It is late!

Cinderella must go.

She runs down the stairs.

She loses a glass slipper.

The magic stops.
Cinderella's dress
and coach change back.
She has one glass slipper.

The Prince's true love
is gone.

He has her glass slipper.

The Prince's father
wants to find her.

Lady Tremaine locks
Cinderella in her room.
She does not want
the Prince to find her.

Cinderella's friends
get the key to her room.
They unlock the door.

Cinderella tries on
the glass slipper.
It fits!
She is the Prince's
true love!

Cinderella
and the Prince
get married.
They live happily
ever after!

THE LITTLE MERMAID

by Ruth Homberg

illustrated by the Disney Storybook Artists

Random House 🏠 New York

Ariel is a mermaid.

She is also a princess.

Flounder is her friend.

Scuttle is her friend, too.
He teaches Ariel
about humans.

Ariel dreams of life
above the sea.

King Triton
is Ariel's father.
He is angry
with Ariel.

He does not
trust humans.
He wants Ariel
to stay home.

At night,
Ariel swims
above the water.
There is a storm.

She sees a human.

His name is Prince Eric.

He falls off a ship!

Ariel saves Eric.

Ariel sings
to Eric.
She falls in love
with him.

Ursula is an evil witch.

She takes Ariel's voice.

She gives Ariel legs.

Ariel must kiss Eric.

She has three days.

If they do not kiss,
she will lose her legs
and her voice forever.

Ariel is human!

She can live on land.

She loves her new legs.

Ariel's friends help her.

Scuttle makes

her a dress.

Eric is looking

for the girl

who sang to him.

He thinks it is Ariel.

But she has no voice.

Eric brings Ariel
to the palace.

She combs her hair
with a fork!
Eric laughs.
He likes Ariel.

Eric and Ariel
go on a boat ride.
They almost kiss.

Ursula's eels tip

the boat over!

Ursula does not want
Eric to kiss Ariel.
She changes herself.
She uses Ariel's voice.

Eric loves her voice.
He thinks he is in love
with Ursula!

Eric is going
to marry Ursula!
Scuttle finds out
about her trick.

Scuttle and his friends
stop Ursula.

Ariel's voice is back!

It is too late.

She turns

into a mermaid again.

Ursula laughs.

She turns

into a huge monster!

Eric stops her for good.

King Triton wants Ariel

to be happy.

He makes her
human again.

Eric loves Ariel.
Now they can be
together forever.

Eric and Ariel live
happily ever after!

Tangled

Outside My Window

by Melissa Lagonegro

illustrated by Jean-Paul Orpiñas,
Studio IBOIX,
and the Disney Storybook Artists

Random House 🏠 New York

Rapunzel is a princess
with magic golden hair.

One night,
Mother Gothel takes
baby Rapunzel!
She wants
Rapunzel's magic hair
to make her young.

Rapunzel grows up
in a tower.
Her hair
is very long.

Mother Gothel uses
Rapunzel's hair
to climb the tower.
Rapunzel does not know
that Mother Gothel
kidnapped her.

Rapunzel sees lights
in the sky every year.
She loves to paint them.
She wants to go
to the lights.

But Mother Gothel
says it is not safe.

Flynn is a thief.
Guards want
to catch him.
He must hide.

By Order of the KING
WANTED!
1,000 CROWNS REWARD!

THIEF

Flynn finds
Rapunzel's tower.
He can hide there!

Rapunzel finds Flynn
in her tower.
She is scared!

She catches him.
Then she hides him
in the closet.

Rapunzel still wants
to go to the lights.
She asks Flynn
to take her.

Then she will
let him go.
Flynn says yes.

Rapunzel leaves the tower!

Mother Gothel cannot
find Rapunzel.
She thinks Flynn
kidnapped her.
Mother Gothel is angry.

Rapunzel goes to a pub.

She makes new friends.

She likes
the outside world!

The guards find
Flynn and Rapunzel.
Their new friends
help them escape!

Rapunzel and Flynn
find a cave.
Water fills the cave.
They cannot see!
Rapunzel uses
her magic hair.
It glows and shows
the way out.

Rapunzel sees the kingdom.

Rapunzel sees a picture.

It shows the King,

the Queen,

and the lost princess.

The Princess has

the same green eyes

as Rapunzel.

Rapunzel sees the lights!
She and Flynn fall
in love.

But Flynn sails away.

Rapunzel is sad.

She goes back
to the tower
with Mother Gothel.

Rapunzel learns that she
is the lost princess!
Mother Gothel
sent Flynn away.

Rapunzel wants to leave.
But Mother Gothel
will not let her go.

Flynn comes
to save Rapunzel!
He cuts her hair.
The magic is gone.
Mother Gothel turns
to dust!

But Flynn is hurt.

Rapunzel cries.

Her tears heal Flynn!

Everyone welcomes
Princess Rapunzel home.
They all live
happily ever after!

STEP INTO READING®

DISNEY·PIXAR

A MOTHER'S LOVE

by Melissa Lagonegro

illustrated by Maria Elena Naggi
and Studio IBOIX

Random House 🏠 New York

Princess Merida is late.
The royal family waits.

Merida's mother

is the queen.

The queen teaches Merida
how to be a princess.
She shows Merida
how to play the harp.
Merida is bored.

Merida wants

to play with her sword.

The queen tells Merida
she must marry
the son of a lord.

It is her job
as the princess.
Merida is mad!

Merida gets ready
to meet some lords' sons.
She wears a fancy gown.
The queen is proud.

Merida is sad.
She does not want
to get married.

The young lords
will shoot arrows
at a target.

The best shooter
will marry the princess.

Merida joins the game.

She is the best.

She wins!

Now no one
can marry Merida.
The queen is mad.

The queen wants Merida
to get married.

Merida says no.

She cuts

the family tapestry.

Merida runs away.
She meets a Witch.
She asks the Witch
to change the queen.

The Witch makes a cake
that holds a spell.
The spell
will change the queen.

Merida returns
to the castle.
The queen eats
the spell cake.

The cake
changes the queen—
into a bear!
Merida did not want this.

Merida and her mother
look for the Witch.
They need her
to break the spell.
But the Witch is gone!

Merida and her mother
go fishing.
They have fun.

Merida and her mother
meet a mean bear.
They run back
to the castle.

Merida wants
to help her mother.
She wants to mend
the family tapestry.

Merida tells the lords
she will marry
one of their sons.
The queen stops her.
She wants Merida
to be happy.

The men chase the queen
from the castle.

The queen is in trouble.

No one knows

she is the bear!

Merida protects her.

The mean bear returns!
The queen
protects Merida.
The two bears fight.

Merida fixes

the torn tapestry.

She and her mother hug.

The tapestry covers them.

The queen is
human again!
Love has
broken the spell.

Merida and the queen
will always be
mother and daughter.
Now they are friends,
too.